HAY FOR MY OX

and other stories

A first reading book for Waldorf schools

Edited by Isabel Wyatt and Joan Rudel

Floris Books

Original layout by Arne Klingborg
Illustrations by Auvikki Mikkola
First published in 1968 by The Lanthorn Press
This edition published in 2012 by Floris Books
Second printing 2015
© The Lanthorn Press 1968

"The Rain" by W. H. Davies, from The Complete Poems of W. H. Davies
© Jonathan Cape Limited, reprinted by permission of Jonathan Cape
Limited and Wesleyan University Press; "The Hare" by Rose Fyleman
reprinted by permission of the Estate of Rose Fyleman, represented by
The Society of Authors; "Some One" by Walter de la Mare reprinted by
permission of the Literary Trustees of Walter de la Mare, represented by
The Society of Authors.

British Library CIP data available
ISBN 978-086315-913-8
Printed in China through Asia Pacific Offset Ltd

Contents

Hay For My Ox

An old farmer had two sons, Cross-Patch and Jeff.

Cross-Patch was a man.

But Jeff was still a boy.

Jeff had a little red ox.

This little red ox was as dear to him as if he were his son.

And so, in a way, he was, because the old farmer had let Jeff bring up the little red ox by hand.

The old farmer died.

Cross-Patch now had the farm.

"Cross-Patch," said Jeff, "I need hay for my little red ox."

"You will get no hay from me," said Cross-Patch.

Jeff told his little red ox, "We must go and find hay for you."

And off he went, to find hay for his little red ox.

His little red ox went with him.

They went a little way; they went a long way.

The way led at last to a neat little farm.

Jeff went into the farmyard.

His little red ox went with him.

Jeff saw stalls for ten horses, and the horses in them.

He saw sheds for ten cows, and the cows in them.

He saw sties for ten pigs, and the pigs in them.

He saw a barn for ten carts, and the carts in them.

And by the wall of the barn he saw a big blue hay cart, full of fresh, sweet hay.

It was so full that the hay spilled out.

It was the kind of hay cart the little red ox dreamed of in his sleep.

By it stood an old man.

He was as plump and red as a robin.

"What are you looking for, farmer's boy?" he said. "Are you looking for gold? Are you looking for happiness?"

"No, sir," said Jeff.

"I am looking for hay for my little red ox."

"If you can pass a test," said the Robin-Man, "you can have all the hay you need for the rest of your life. What do you think of that?"

"Good, and better than good, sir," said Jeff.

The Robin-Man led Jeff to a stable.

The little red ox went with them.

The stable had big bolts and bars.

In it were five colts.

One colt had black hoofs.

One colt had white hoofs.

One colt had green hoofs.

One colt had gold hoofs.

One colt had wet hoofs.

"I will lock you in with them," said the Robin-Man. "If you can tell me how they get such hoofs, this neat little farm will be yours,

and the hay for your little red ox. What do you think of that?"

"Good, and better than good, sir," said Jeff.

He let the Robin-Man lock him in with the colts.

He lay down in the straw to sleep.

His little red ox lay down with him.

"Little Red Ox," said Jeff. "We have four eyes, you and I. Two eyes can shut, and two can stay open until the colts stir."

The two eyes that shut were Jeff's.

The little red ox kept his open.

Jeff slept.

But when he felt Little Red Ox butt him, up he sprang.

He saw the five colts thrust back the big bolts and bars.

He saw them rush out with a stamp of the hoof and a flash of the eye and a sweep of the mane and a toss of the tail.

He ran out too.

And his little red ox went with him.

Jeff saw Black-Hoof swoop into the soil.

He saw Wet-Hoof swoop into the brook.

He saw Green-Hoof fly up to run on the treetops.

He saw White-Hoof fly up to play in the clouds.

He saw Gold-Hoof fly up to kick the stars.

Then all five colts came back.

They all ran to the blue hay cart.

They all piled hay on hay until it lay in banks of spilled gold.

Jeff went to find the Robin-Man.

His little red ox went with him.

Jeff told the Robin-Man, "Black-Hoof's hoofs are black with soil. Wet-Hoof's hoofs are wet from the brook. Green-Hoof's hoofs are green from the treetops. White-Hoof's hoofs are white from the clouds. Gold-Hoof's hoofs are gold with stardust. I need all five if I am to have hay for my little red ox. What do you think of that?"

"Good, and better than good," said the Robin-Man. "The colts and the neat little farm are yours. *And* the hay for your little red ox."

So Jeff got the colts, and the neat little farm, *and* the hay for his little red ox.

He was as happy as happy can be.

And so was his little red ox.

Brother Ox and Brother Ass

Brother Ox and Brother Ass slept in one stable.

All day long, Brother Ox had to pull an ox-cart for the farmer, to bring in his corn and hay.

Tim was the farmer's young son.

Brother Ass was Tim's pet.

So Brother Ass had no farm tasks to do.

He had all day to kick up his heels in the sun.

Tim was born under a lucky star.

If you are born under that lucky star, you can tell what a dog or a cat or an ox or an ass says.

But it has to be when that lucky star is in the sky.

Tim saw his lucky star in the sky when he went to bed.

He got up to look at it.

He saw the stable with its roof of reeds.

The wind had torn a gap in the roof.

Tim saw that this gap was lit up.

So out to the stable Tim went on the tips of his toes.

The farmer had left a ladder by the stable wall, to mend the gap in the roof next day.

Up the ladder, as fast as an adder, went Tim, to look through the gap in the roof.

He saw that the farmer had left his stable lamp hanging on the wall, still lit.

He saw Brother Ox and Brother Ass, each in his stall.

"Brother Ass," said Brother Ox, "how lucky you are! You have no farm tasks to do. You have all day to kick up your heels in the sun. But all day *I* have to pull an ox-cart, full of corn and hay."

"Brother Ox," said Brother Ass, "why do you do it?

When they try to put you in the harness, do not let them.

You must tramp and stamp and butt and toss and rip up the grass. Then you, too, will not need to do farm tasks.

You, too, can have all day to kick up your heels in the sun."

"I will try it, Brother Ass," said Brother Ox.

Next day, the farmer said to Tim, "Tim, keep away from Brother Ox. When I went to put him in the harness, he went mad."

"Brother Ass told him to do that," said Tim.

And he told the farmer all that Brother Ox and Brother Ass had said.

"Well, well, well!" said the farmer. "What trick will Brother Ass get up to next?"

The farmer went to the stable.

He put Brother Ass in the harness of the ox-cart.

All day Brother Ass had to pull it, full of corn and hay.

All day Brother Ox was free to kick up his heels in the sun.

As soon as Tim's lucky star lit up the sky that night, Tim went out to the stable on the tips of his toes.

Up the ladder, as fast as an adder, he went, to look through the gap in the roof.

"Brother Ass," said Brother Ox, "I did just as you told me. And what a day I have had! All day I have been free to kick up my heels in the sun."

"Brother Ox," said Brother Ass, "I bring you such bad news. The farmer says that if you are too mad to pull the ox-cart, he may as well kill you."

"No! Did he?" cried Brother Ox. "Then I have to pull it. I do not want to die just yet."

So, next day, when the farmer went to put him in the harness, Brother Ox was meek and gentle.

"Tim," said the farmer, "we must find a farm task for Brother Ass to do. If we do not, he will find new tricks to play on us."

"Let me go to the mill with the corn for Miller to grind," said

Tim. "I can put the corn in two bags, and sling them on the back of Brother Ass. And that can be his farm task."

"Yes, do that," said the farmer.

So Tim did.

"I wish I had not told Brother Ox to go mad," said Brother Ass. "I never seem free now to kick up my heels in the sun!"

The Hare

Between the valley and the hill

   There sat a little hare;

It nibbled at the grass until

   The ground was nearly bare.

And when the ground was nearly bare

   It rested in the sun;

A hunter came and saw it there

   And shot it with his gun.

It thought it must be dead, be dead,

   But, wonderful to say,

It found it was alive instead

   And quickly ran away.

Where Go the Boats?

Dark brown is the river,

Golden is the sand.

It flows along forever,

With trees on either hand.

Green leaves a-floating,

Castles of the foam,

Boats of mine a-boating –

Where will all come home?

On goes the river

And out past the mill,

Away down the valley,

Away down the hill.

Away down the river,

A hundred miles or more,

Other little children

Shall bring my boats ashore.

R. L. Stevenson

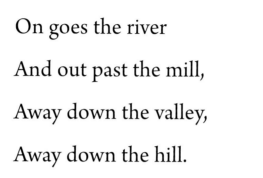

The Prince Who Kept Pigs

Prince Harry was the son of a king. When Prince Harry was still a boy, the king died. His enemy won the land.

The new king sent Prince Harry to Hog Rock. On Hog Rock an old swineherd kept the king's pigs. Prince Harry had to help him.

On each side of Hog Rock there was sea all the way to the sky.

But one clear day, Prince Harry saw cliffs a long way off.

He said to the old swineherd, "What land is that?"

And the old swineherd told him, "It is a land *not* to try to get to. In that land all men are afraid of a mad wild boar."

Prince Harry said to his pigs,

"I *will* try to get to that land, mad boar or no mad boar. For if I can do that, I will be free."

But how was he going to get to that land? It was much too far to swim.

And he had no boat to float in. And he had no tools.

The old swineherd kept the sows and the small pigs in sties near his hut. Each day he sent Prince Harry out into the wood with the big hogs that had to get fat.

All day long, the hogs fed on the nuts that fell from the trees.

When they saw Prince Harry pick up a stick, they ran to him with grunts of joy. They stood still for him to scratch them with his stick on the back and ears. Then they lay and slept.

In this way, seven years went by. Prince Harry was now a man.

Then, one day, the sea washed up a log on the sands.

The old swineherd slept each day at noon. So now, every day at noon, Prince Harry left his hogs to feed in the woods.

He ran down to the log on the sands.

He took sharp flints. With them, bit by bit, he dug a boat out of the log. He had a branch for a mast. He had two sticks for oars.

But he still had to stay on Hog Rock until a west wind blew.

Day after day after day, the wind blew all ways but that way.

At last, one day, a brisk west wind sprang up.

Prince Harry left his hogs to feed in the wood. Down to the sands he ran.

Push, pull; push, pull; push, pull – splash – and his boat floated on the sea.

He hung his coat on the mast to catch that brisk west wind.

He took an oar in each hand. And over the sea he sped.

Rock roll; rock roll; rock roll; tip toss; tip toss; tip toss.

On he went, with the help of that brisk west wind.

Hog Rock was soon a dot in the sea at his back. The cliffs in front of him grew clear. The cliffs in front of him grew near.

Now he saw the walls of a town on the cliff. Now he saw a wood. Then the sea fell on him.

It flung him up. It flung him down. It flung him on the sands at the foot of the cliff.

People saw him from the walls of the town. They ran down the cliff path to him.

They held him up by the heels, to pour the sea out of him.

They put him flat on the sands, to pump and thump the sea out of him.

Soon Prince Harry sat up.

He said to the men, "Do you still live in fear of a mad wild boar in this land?"

"We do," they said.

"Then take me to your king," said Prince Harry.

"We have no king," they told him. "Our king has just died. His only child is now our queen. She will marry the man who kills the mad wild boar."

"Then bring me a sack and a spear," said Prince Harry.

He took the sack and the spear. He went up the cliff. He went into the wood.

In the wood, he went from tree to tree, to pick nuts, until his sack was full.

The mad wild boar smelled the smell of man in the wood. His eyes went red. Froth fell from his lips.

The mad wild boar ran after the smell of man – dash, clash, crash, splash, smash.

Prince Harry fled up a tree. The mad wild boar sped at the tree.

His tusks were long. His tusks were strong. At each rush of that mad wild boar, Prince Harry felt the tree rock. At each rush of that mad wild boar, Prince Harry felt the twigs thrash.

He threw down nuts from his sack. As soon as the wild boar saw the nuts, he stood and ate them. Prince Harry threw down more nuts, and still more nuts, until he had thrown down all he had.

At last the wild boar was full. Then Prince Harry held onto the tree with his legs and his left hand. He bent down to scratch the back and ears of the mad wild boar with the tip of his spear.

Grunt, grunt, grunt, went the happy mad wild boar. He stood still for the tip of the spear to scratch him. And at last he lay down and slept.

Then Prince Harry thrust his spear deep into the wild boar's neck.

And the people of that land were no longer afraid.

Prince Harry went back to the town on the cliff. He sent men to drag the wild boar in, for all to see.

The queen ran out of the town to meet Prince Harry. She held her hands out to him.

"It is *your* town, and *your* land, now," she told him. "From this day you are its king. But tell me how you did it. When other men went to kill him, the mad wild boar attacked them."

"They did not know all that *I* know," said Prince Harry. "They had not looked after pigs for seven years!"

Mark and his Lamp

A king had ten sons. The last son was still a boy. He was Prince Mark. The king died. He left his land to his ten sons.

But the nine sons who were men said, "Why should we let Mark have a part of the land? He is still a boy. Let us send him to look for luck in far-off lands."

So they put a big hat on his head, to keep off the sun.

They put a big bag on his back, full of crusts for the journey.

They put a big staff in his hand, with a steel tip on it.

They put big rag boots on his feet.

And they sent him to look for luck in far-off lands.

Mark set off. He went on and on until four roads met.

He did not know the way to go. So he sat with his back to a tree and a crust from his bag in his hand.

A little old man went past. He was bent over. A lamp hung and swung from his hand.

"I wish *I* had a crust," said the little old man.

"Have one, little old man," said Mark.

And he put a crust from his bag in the old man's hand.

The little old man sat by Mark, with *his* back to a tree, and a crust in *his* hand.

Munch, crunch, went the little old man.

Munch, crunch, went Mark.

"How old are you, little old man?" said Mark.

"Not as old as all that," said the little old man. "Only five hundred years old."

"Then, little old man," said Mark, "can you tell me the best land to look for luck in?"

And the little old man told him,

"You must go as far as the wind can blow. You must go as far as the rain can wet. You must go as far as the sea can flow. You must go as far as the sun can run."

"And how will I tell when I get as far as that, little old man?" said Mark.

"This lamp will tell you," said the little old man. "This lamp will go out when you get to the end of your journey. Then you must put down roots, and grow."

"Can you show me the way, little old man?" said Mark.

"Hold up the lamp," said the little old man.

Mark held up the lamp. It lit up the way to the left.

"That is the way to the land you seek," said the little old man. "And that is the way you must go."

So that was the way Mark went. He went in the day; he went in the dark. Not a wink of sleep, not a blink of sleep did he get. The little old man's lamp lit up his way.

"Walk on, walk on," sang Mark. "I must go as far as the wind can blow. I must go as far as the rain can wet. I must go as far as the sea can flow. I must go as far as the sun can run."

On and on he went, until his big bag had no crusts left in it.

On and on he went, until the steel tip of his staff was worn down to the wood.

On and on he went, until his big hat hung from his head in wisps.

On and on he went, until his big rag boots hung from his feet in shreds.

And still the little old man's lamp lit up his way.

He went as far as the wind can blow. He went as far as the rain can wet. He went as far as the sea can flow. He went as far as the sun can run.

And then his lamp went out.

Mark went to the king of that land. The king of that land was little and old.

"I think I must be at the end of my journey, little old king," said Mark.

"I need a boy who is at the end of his journey," said the little old king. "But he must be the son of a king."

"That is just what I am, little old king," said Mark.

He did not look like the son of a king, with his worn staff in his hand, and the bag on his back, and his big hat that hung in wisps, and his big rag boots that hung in shreds.

"I will tell you if you *are* the son of a king when you have slept," said the little old king.

So Mark went off to bed. As soon as he put down his head, he slept and he slept and he slept.

Then the little old king went in on tiptoe. Under each of Mark's four bed-posts he slid an ivy leaf. Then the little old king went out on tiptoe. And still Mark slept and slept and slept.

"Did you sleep well?" said the little old king, next day.

"So well, little old king," said Mark, "that I did not feel you put me in a new bed."

"But I did not put you in a new bed," said the little old king. "Why do you think I did?"

"I will tell you, little old king," said Mark. "When I sat up to rub the sleep from my eyes, the bed felt less low than the bed I went to sleep in."

"How much less low?" said the little old king.

"Oh, a lot, little old king," said Mark. "As much as a flat ivy leaf."

Then the little old king said, "That tells me that you *are* the son of a king. And *I* will tell *you* why I need one. I have no son. I need a king's son to bring up as *my* son, to be king of this land when I die. Are you willing?"

"Willing and more than willing, little old king," said Mark.

Then he knew that this *was* the end of his journey. And he did as the little old man had told him – he put down roots, and grew.

Ripe Plums in Spring

Bob was as strong as an ox. But Bob was as poor as a wren.

"One day I will ask the king to let me work for him," said Bob. "Kings need strong men. But how can I get to see the king when I am dressed in rags?"

Bob went into the wood one day in spring. The trees were full of green buds. But one tree was full of ripe plums.

"Ripe plums in spring?" cried Bob. "I have never seen such a thing before! I will pick them for the king. Then I can get to see him, and he might let me work for him."

So Bob took off his hat to put the ripe plums in. When the hat was full, he put green weeds on top. The green weeds kept the ripe plums fresh.

Then Bob set off with his hat of ripe plums to go to the king.

He went to the king's gate. At the king's gate sat the king's guard.

The king's guard saw Bob's rags.

"Go away, beggar!" cried the king's guard. "Or I will cuff your ears until you see stars!"

"Sir, let me in," said Bob. "I bring a gift for the king."

The guard lifted up the green weeds from the top of the hat.

He saw it was full of ripe plums.

"Ripe plums in spring?" cried the guard. "I have never seen such a thing before! The king will pay you well for this gift. I will let you in. But you must give me a third of what you get for them."

"You shall have it," said Bob.

So the king's guard let Bob in at the king's gate. And Bob went on to the door of the king's hall.

At the door of the king's hall sat the king's door-keeper. The king's door-keeper saw Bob's rags.

"Go away, beggar!" cried the king's door-keeper. "Or you will feel your ribs rattle!"

"Sir, let me in," said Bob. "I bring a gift for the king."

The door-keeper lifted up the green weeds from the top of the hat. He saw it was full of ripe plums.

"Ripe plums in spring?" cried the door-keeper. "I have never seen such a thing before! The king will pay you well for this gift. I will let you in. But you must give me third of what you get for them."

"You shall have it," said Bob.

So the king's door-keeper let Bob into the king's hall. And Bob went on to the door of the king's room.

At the door of the king's room sat the king's groom. The king's groom saw Bob's rags.

"Go away, beggar!" cried the king's groom. "Or I will sweep you off your legs!"

"Sir, let me in," said Bob. "I bring a gift for the king."

The groom lifted up the green weeds from the top of the hat. He saw it was full of ripe plums.

"Ripe plums in spring?" cried the groom. "I have never seen such a thing before! The king will pay you well for this gift. I will let you in. But you must give me a third of what you get for them."

"You shall have it," said Bob.

So the king's groom let Bob into the king's room. Bob went to the king. He bent to his feet.

"Lord King," said Bob, "I bring you this gift."

The king lifted up the green weeds from the top of the hat.

He saw it was full of ripe plums.

"Ripe plums in spring?" cried the king. "I have never seen such a thing before! It is the best gift. What gift do *you* want from *me*?"

"Lord King, three blows, to give as I wish," said Bob.

"They are yours," said the king.

"Then, Lord King," said Bob, "send for your groom, your door-keeper and your guard."

The king sent for them. They stood in front of him.

Bob went to the king's guard.

"Sir," he said, "I give you your third of what I got for my plums."

Whish-swish went Bob's fist. That guard got such a cuff on the ear that he saw stars.

Bob went to the king's door-keeper.

"Sir," he said, "I give you your third of what I got for my plums."

Whish-swish went Bob's fist. That door-keeper got such a blow that he felt his ribs rattle.

Bob went to the king's groom.

"Good sir," he said, "I give you your third of what I got for my plums."

Whish-swish went Bob's fist. That groom got such a blow that it swept him off his legs.

"Goodness me!" cried the king. "The man is as strong as an ox! Will you work for me? Kings need strong men like you."

And so Bob got his wish.

Spring

Sound the flute!

Now it's mute.

Birds delight

Day and night

Nightingale

In the dale,

Lark in sky,

Merrily

Merrily, merrily, to welcome in the year.

Little boy,

Full of joy;

Little girl,

Sweet and small;

Cock does crow,

So do you;

Merry voice,

Infant noise,

Merrily, merrily, to welcome in the year.

Little lamb,

Here I am;

Come and lick

My white neck;

Let me pull

Your soft wool;

Let me kiss

Your soft face:

Merrily, merrily, to welcome in the year.

William Blake

Some One

Some one came knocking

At my wee, small door;

Some one came knocking

I'm sure – sure – sure;

I listened, I opened,

I looked from left to right,

But nought there was a-stirring

In the still dark night;

Only the busy beetle

Tap-tapping in the wall,

Only from the forest

The screeching owl call,

Only the cricket whistling

While the dew drops fall,

So I know not who came knocking,

At all, at all, at all.

Walter De La Mare

The Elves' Dance

Round about, round about

In a fair ring-a,

Thus we dance, thus we dance

And thus we sing-a,

Trip and go, to and fro

Over this green-a,

All about, in and out,

For our brave Queen-a.

Anonymous

The Tree of Three Cries

An old monk had his hut in the wild Welsh land, to teach its wild Welsh people. Baglan was a boy who lived with him, to help him.

When Baglan grew up, the old monk said to him, "Baglan, you must do as I do. You must go to a new place in this wild Welsh land. You, too, must teach its wild Welsh people."

"How will I know the way to go?" said Baglan.

"A *baglan* shall tell you," said the old monk.

And he put a crook in Baglan's hand, because in Welsh, *baglan* is a crook.

And the old monk told him, "At each crossroads, you must stand the crook up. And the way the crook falls, go that way. That will be the way to the place you seek; and that is the way you must go."

"How can I tell when I reach the place I seek?" said Baglan.

And the old monk told him, "When you reach a tree of three cries, that is the place you seek."

So Baglan set off with his crook.

He went on three legs. At each crossroads he stood the crook up; and the way the crook fell, that was the way he went.

"That is the way to the place I seek," he said. "And that is the way I must go."

His crook led him at last to the top of a big hill. A big tree stood at the top of this hill.

At the bottom of the tree was a wild sow with ten little pigs. At the top of the tree was a rooks' nest. Wild bees swept in and out of a gap in the trunk of the tree.

As Baglan went to the tree, the sow and her ten little pigs ran to meet him and to greet him with a *grunt, grunt, grunt.*

The rooks flew on big black wings to meet him and to greet him with a *caw, caw, caw.*

The wild bees swept to meet him and to greet him with a *buzz, buzz, buzz.*

Baglan stood his crook at the foot of the tree. It did not fall this way or that way. It just stood.

"This must be the tree of three cries," said Baglan. "This is the place I seek; and this is the place I must stay in."

Baglan did not think the top of a big hill was a good place to build his hut. So he went to the bottom of the hill.

Each day, he put up a bit of his hut. But the bit he put up each day fell down, *smash*, as soon as he slept.

So he went back to the top of the hill.

The pigs, big and little, dug up rocks at the bottom of the tree for him, with a *grunt, grunt, grunt* of joy.

The rooks flew off each day, to bring back crusts for him, with a *caw, caw, caw* of joy.

The bees swept out from the tree trunk each day with bits of sweet honeycomb for him, with a *buzz, buzz, buzz* of joy.

"How blessed am I," said Baglan, "in this tree of three cries!"

So Baglan built his hut at the bottom of the tree.

He left a gap at the bottom of the wall of the hut. This was for the wild sow and her ten little pigs to go in and out.

He left a gap six feet up in the wall of the hut. This was for the wild bees to go into the tree trunk.

He left a gap in the roof, at the top of the tree. This was for the rooks to go into their nest.

A wild Welsh man of that wild Welsh land saw Baglan's hut. He went back and told his friends what he had seen. The wild Welsh people went to see Baglan – three of them, six of them, ten of them, twenty of them, fifty of them.

Baglan sat by his hut to teach them.

Under the tree of the three cries, the wild Welsh people sat still, for Baglan to teach them.

The wild pigs lay still at his feet, for Baglan to teach them, too.

The wild bees hung still in the tree trunk, for Baglan to teach them, too.

The rooks sat still in the treetop, for Baglan to teach them, too.

At this tree of the three cries, wild rooks and wild bees and wild pigs and wild Welsh people met day by day, for Baglan to bless them.

How Sheep Got Sheep Bells

All day the sheep went up on the hills, to eat the sweet hill grass and get fat. At dusk, Otto the Shepherd went up with his crook, to bring them all back to the sheepfold.

The sheep went into the sheepfold. But Black-Sheep was not with them. So Otto the Shepherd took his crook, and went back to find her.

The mist was thick now on the hills. To and fro, to and fro in the mist went Otto the Shepherd, until he had lost his way. Then – one step – and he was out of the mist. Two steps, and his feet were on a sheep track. Three steps, and with a cry of joy he saw a star glow low in the sky.

"But *is* it a star?" said Otto the Shepherd. "Or is it a lamp on the hilltop?"

The sheep track led him up and up, to a cleft in the rock on the hilltop. The star was glowing in a gap in that steep wall of rock.

Out of that gap blew a cry, "Baa-aa-aa!"

Otto the Shepherd bent to look in.

He saw a big cave, lit by the glow of gold. In it, dressed all in gold, a king lay deep asleep. His men, dressed in gold and steel, lay with him, row after row.

Black-Sheep stood next to them.

"Black-Sheep!" Otto the Shepherd cried to her.

"Baa-aa-aa!" she cried back.

And with a jump of joy she ran to him.

It was a steep jump for Black-Sheep up to the gap. Otto the Shepherd held out his crook to help her up. It struck a big golden bell that hung over the gap.

Clink, clang, clink, clang, the bell rang out, with a clash of gold on gold. The cave shook with its clash. Otto the Shepherd felt the hill rock.

In the cave, the gold-dressed king jumped to his feet. All his men jumped up with him. The cave rang with the clash of gold on gold. The cave rang with the clang of steel on steel.

"Who rang the bell?" cried the king. "Does the land need my help?"

Otto the Shepherd cried back, "Not yet! Not yet! Sleep on! Sleep on! Sleep on!"

"Sleep on! Sleep on!" said the king to his men. "The land does not need us yet."

The king went back to sleep. All his men went back to sleep.

"So that is a bell, is it?" said Otto the Shepherd to Black-Sheep.

He bent in the gap, to get a good look. He had not seen a bell before then. There were no bells in his land in those days.

"Black-Sheep," he said, "if I hang a bell like that from your neck, it will help me to find you when you next get lost. What do you say?"

"Baa-aa-aa!" said Black-Sheep.

Otto the Shepherd left the hilltop. Black-Sheep went with him.

By now the moon was up. It lit the sheep track that led them back to the sheepfold.

Next day, Otto the Shepherd saw that Black-Sheep's wool was thick with gold dust. A tuft of that wool, sold now and then, gave him everything he needed.

He took a tuft to the blacksmith.

"This is to pay for a bell to hang from Black-Sheep's neck," Otto the Shepherd told him.

"A bell?" said the blacksmith. "What is a bell?"

Otto the Shepherd told him.

Otto the Shepherd got his bell. He hung it from Black-Sheep's neck.

Chink-chink, clink-clink went the bell when the sheep went up on the hills to eat.

Chink-chink, clink-clink went the bell, and led Otto the Shepherd to Black-Sheep when she got lost.

And that is how sheep got sheep bells.

The Giant and the Child

Long, long ago, there was a giant as bad as he was big. He was as big as six men; he was as bad as ten. He was as strong as ten men, too.

He told a brave monk this, one day. But the brave monk did not bat an eyelash.

The brave monk said, "It is good to be strong, if we help men with this gift. The king who is *my* king did; and no one is as strong as him."

"If I am less strong than he is," said the giant, "he is fit to be *my* king, and I, too, will help men. How can I do this?"

The bold monk told him, "You can carry people over the river on your back. It is too big and too deep and too fast for them to cross."

"And when will I see my strong king?" said the giant.

"When you do not expect to see him," said the monk.

"Then who will tell me who he is?" said the giant.

"You will not need to be told," said the monk.

"Shall *I* tell *him* who I am?" said the giant.

"*He* will tell *you*," said the monk.

The giant cut the branches off a tree and used the trunk as a staff, to help him over the river.

He went to the bank of the river. At its edge he piled tree trunk on top of tree trunk until he had a hut to rest in.

He hung a big bell on the wall of the hut, for people to call him. He also hung a long string for them to pull, to ring the bell.

When people rang the bell, *ding-dong, ding-dong,* he went to them.

He bent his long legs; he bent his long back; and he swung them up on his back.

And in seven giant steps he took them over the river.

One winter's day, it was cold as cold and wet as wet. The wind was wild. The river went by with a rush. It threw up spray at the giant's hut.

"No one will want to cross on such a wild day," said the giant. "I can stay snug in bed, and get a good long sleep."

He had just got snug in his bed when the big bell rang. It did not ring *ding-dong, ding-dong;* it rang a small, small *ting-a-ling-a-ling.*

The giant got up from his bed. He took his big, strong staff in his big, strong hand. And he went out into the cold, wet wind.

And who stood by the bell string?

A small, small child!

The wind swung that small, small child. The spray stung that small, small child. But that small, small child just clung to the bell string; and he stood as still as still.

"Can you carry me over the river, good Giant?" said the small, small child.

"On my hand," said the giant.

"On your back will be best, good Giant," said the small, small child. "I may not be as small as you think."

The giant swung the small, small child up on his back. And into the river, the deep, cold, fast, wild river, the giant went.

He took one giant step in the river. It felt as if he had no one on his back.

"What a small, small child," said the giant, "this small, small child is!"

He took two giant steps in the river. Now he felt the child big on his back.

"This small, small child," said the giant, "must be a man!"

He took three giant steps in the river. Now he bent under the child on his back.

"This small, small child," said the giant, "must be a tree!"

He took four giant steps in the river. The child on his back bent him until he clung to his staff.

"This small, small child," said the giant, "must be a hill!"

He took five giant steps in the river. The child was now so big that the giant sank even lower.

"This small, small child," said the giant, "must be the sky!"

He took six giant steps in the river. The child on his back lit up all the land.

"This small, small child," said the giant, "must be the sun!"

He took seven giant steps in the river. He bent his long legs; he bent his long back; he bent his long neck; and he put the small, small child, still dry, on the bank.

On the bank the winter grass was as fresh as if it was spring time.

The winter trees were as full of buds as if it was spring time.

"This small, small child," said the giant, "must be my king!"

"Yes, I am your king, good Giant," said the small, small child. "And from now on, *you* are Christopher, He-who-carries-Christ."

And from then on, the giant *was* Christopher.

Two Prayers of Olden Days

God be in my head

And in my understanding,

God be in my eyes

And in my looking,

God be in my mouth

And in my speaking,

God be in my heart

And in my thinking,

God be at my end

And at my departing.

Matthew, Mark, Luke and John,

Bless the bed that I lie on,

Four corners to my bed,

Four angels round my head;

One to watch and one to pray

And two to bear my soul away.

Anonymous

King Vincent and Lord Tom-Tit

Lord Tom-Tit was a small brown bird, just one inch tall. He and Lady Tom-Tit got food from King Vincent's rye field.

But they did not *eat* King Vincent's rye. They kept it free from greenfly.

To and fro they flew over the weeds at the side of King Vincent's rye field. *Peck*, they went at the seeds of the weeds, as they clung to them upside down.

One day, King Vincent went to look at his rye field. He saw the tall weeds at the side of it.

He said to his men, "How long have weeds grown at the side of my rye field?"

"So long, King," said his men, "that no one can say *how* long."

"Then dig them all up by next week," said King Vincent.

"But if we do that, King—" said his men.

But King Vincent cut in, "Do as I told you. My word is final."

Lord Tom-Tit swung upside down in the weeds as King Vincent said all this. He flew back to his nest. He put up his foot to scratch his sad little head.

Lady Tom-Tit sat on the eggs in the nest, soft and snug in her brown feather shawl.

"Why are you sad?" she said. "Why are you scratching your sad little head?"

Lord Tom-Tit told her what King Vincent had just said.

"He will steal the food from our beaks," he said. "And he will steal it out of *his* beak, too. *We* keep his rye free from greenfly. But it is the weeds at the side of the rye field that keep it free from rust disease."

"Did his men not tell him that?" said Lady Tom-Tit.

"They did try to tell him," said Lord Tom-Tit. "But he shut them up with a sharp, *My word is final.* I think I have to jog him and jolt him with a piece of my mind."

"How will you do that?" said Lady Tom-Tit.

And Lord Tom-Tit stood up tall, and told her, "I will go to war with him."

He put on a grass belt. From his belt he hung a long thorn.

He put a nutshell on his head as a helmet, and used another nutshell as a drum. He hung grass from his drum. He had a twig for a drumstick. He held his drumstick with his wing.

He blew Lady Tom-Tit a kiss as she sat on her eggs. And off he went, *hop, hop,* to see King Vincent's men.

His drum swung to and fro on his plump chest. *Bang, bang,* went his drumstick on his drum.

"Why are you banging a drum at us, Lord Tom-Tit?" said King Vincent's men.

And Lord Tom-Tit told them, "To go to war with the king."

"Then we will take you to him," they said. And they led him in to King Vincent.

King Vincent picked him up in his hand.

"So you want to go to war with me, Lord Tom-Tit?" said King Vincent. "But I can hold you in my hand. What if I cut off your cross little head?"

"Do not do that, King Vincent," said Lord Tom-Tit. "And do not cut off the little heads of the weeds at the side of your rye field. If you do, you will get rust disease on your rye, and your rye will die."

"Is this right?" said King Vincent to his men.

"It is, King," they said. "That is why there have been weeds at the side of the rye field so long that no one can say *how* long."

Then King Vincent said to Lord Tom-Tit, "Let us end this war, Lord Tom-Tit. I will not cut off the little heads of the weeds at the side of the rye field. You will be lord of them."

Lord Tom-Tit took his nutshell helmet off his cross little head.

The wind blew his feathers into his eyes.

He said, with a bob and a bow, "Thank you, King Vincent."

And off he flew to his nest.

Lady Tom-Tit still sat on her eggs, soft and snug in her brown feather shawl.

"Did you jog and jolt King Vincent?" she said. "Did you win the war?"

"I did, and I did," Lord Tom-Tit told her. "I shook my drumstick at him. I said, "I hold you in my hand." I said, "What if I cut off your big cross head?" I said, "I must be lord of the weeds at the side of the rye field." I said, "My word is final."

"Did you say all that?" said Lady Tom-Tit. "Take that drum and that belt off, and sit on that twig and sing me a little song. One chick will soon crack through his shell. What shall we call him?"

"Let us call him Vincent, after the king," said Lord Tom-Tit.

And so they did.

Do Not Go Into the Wood

A lark was born on open land, in a nest under a rock.

As he grew up, his mother said to him, "Do not go far to hunt, dear. Stay in your own land. Stay in this open land, and find your food among its rocks."

"Why, Mother?" said the little lark.

And his mother told him, "In your own land, dear, no hawk can catch you. But in a wood, no lark is a match for a hawk. So do not go into the wood."

For a time, the little lark was a good little lark and did as his mother had told him.

Then one day he said, "I *must* go and hunt in the wood!"

So off he went, to hunt in the wood.

In the wood, a hawk saw him. He swooped on him with a thud.

In a flash, the hawk had him tight in his sharp claws.

Then the little lark cried out loud, "Oh, why did I not do as my mother told me?"

The hawk said to him, "What did your mother tell you to do, little lark?"

"To stay and hunt in my own land, and not to go into the wood," cried the little lark.

"And what land is your own land, little lark?" said the hawk.

"The open land, among the rocks," cried the little lark.

"Why did she tell you to stay in your own land, little lark?" said the hawk.

"In my own land no hawk can catch me," cried the little lark.

"Is that so?" said the hawk. "Let us go and try. But you will find I can still catch you, little lark."

So the hawk flew out of the wood, and into the open land, with the little lark still held tight in his sharp claws.

He put the little lark down on a rock. The little lark stood still.

"Catch me, hawk!" he cried.

The hawk made his wings stiff. Flash, flash, he flew at the rock, to snatch up the little lark again in his sharp claws.

"Oh no! The hawk will get me!" cried the little lark.

And with a little bob of his little head, he slid off the rock and down the rock and under the rock, all in one.

And the hawk hit the rock so hard that he was out of breath.

"Well, well!" said the hawk. "I could not catch the little lark, after all!"

And from then on, the little lark did as his mother told him, and he did not go into the wood.

Springtime Rhymes

These two rhymes about springtime and the cuckoo are so old
that the names of the writers are not known.

The Cuckoo

The cuckoo's a bonny bird,

He sings as he flies;

He brings us good tidings;

He tells us no lies.

He drinks the cold water,

To keep his voice clear;

And he'll come again

In the spring of next year.

May Day

Good morning, lords and ladies,

We wish you a happy day,

We hope you'll see our garland,

Because it's the first of May.

The cuckoo sings in April,

The cuckoo sings in May,

The cuckoo sings in June,

In July she flies away.

The cuckoo drinks cold water

To make her sing so clear.

And then she sings Cuckoo –Cuckoo

For three months in the year.

I love my little brother

And sister every day

But I seem to love them better

In the merry month of May.

The Caterpillar

Brown and furry

Caterpillar in a hurry

Take your walk

To the shady leaf or stalk

Or what not,

Which may be the chosen spot.

No toad spy you,

Hovering bird of prey pass by you;

Spin and die,

To live again a butterfly.

Christina Rossetti

The Rain

I hear leaves drinking rain;

I hear rich leaves on top

Giving the poor beneath

Drop after drop;

'Tis a sweet noise to hear

These green leaves drinking near.

And when the sun comes out,

After this rain shall stop,

A wondrous light will fill

Each dark, round drop;

I hope the sun shines bright;

'Twill be a lovely sight.

William H. Davies

The Forktail and the Rams

Two rams met on a cliff path.

"Let me go past," said Ram One.

"Let *me* go past," said Ram Two.

"You must let *me* go past," said Ram One.

"No, *you* must let *me* go past," said Ram Two.

"Get out of my way, you old ram!" said Ram One.

"Get out of *my* way, *you* old ram!" said Ram Two.

They both moved back, to get up speed. Then they ran, and met head-on, *crash, smash.*

"*Now* will you let me go past?" cried Ram One.

"Now will *you* let *me* go past?" cried Ram Two.

Again they both moved back, to get up speed. And again they ran, and met head-on, *crash, smash.*

A forktail bird saw all this as she sat on her eggs in her nest.

"I must stop them, or one of them will crack his skull," she said. So she flew from her nest to stop them.

She cried to Ram One, "Uncle Ram, do not butt heads!"

She cried to Ram Two, "Uncle Ram, be kind and stand still!"

But both rams still kept going.

"What has it to do with you, Forktail?" cried Ram One.

"Get out of the way, Forktail!" cried Ram Two.

To and fro, *crash, smash,* went the rams.

In and out, flip, flap, went the forktail.

Crash, smash, went the rams, just as she got in the way. When she flew free, she had lost the tip of her tail.

"If they won't stop cracking skulls, I should let them keep going," she sighed. "If they crack *my* skull, who will sit on my eggs?"

And *hop, hop, hop,* she went back to sit on her nest.

King Cackle

A king spoke so much that he got the nickname of King Cackle.

A wise man said to him, "Sir, those who talk too much sometimes talk at the wrong time. And bad things can come of that."

But the king made a joke of it.

"Next time you see bad things come of it," he said, "tell me, wise Sir."

Now a turtle lived in the mud by a pond in the hills.

Two wild geese came to that pond.

They met the turtle as they swam on the pond. They became friends.

The time came for the two wild geese to fly home.

They said to the turtle, "Friend Turtle, we do not want to leave you. Why not come home with us?"

"How far away is your home?" said the turtle.

And the wild geese told him, "Only at the other end of the plain."

"That is too far for me," said the turtle. "I can not move very fast."

"Oh, you will not have to walk," said the two wild geese. "You can fly with us."

"But I have no wings," said the turtle.

"You will not need wings," said the two wild geese. "We will get a strong stick, and you can hang onto it by your teeth. And each of us will hold an end of the stick in our beaks as we fly."

"Yes, I can do that," said the turtle.

So the two wild geese got a strong stick. Each of them held an end of the stick in their beak. The turtle held onto the stick with his teeth. And the two wild geese flew into the air.

The wild geese flew fast. The wind went by with a *whoosh*. Soon they had left the hills, and now they flew over the plain.

In the plain stood the city of King Cackle.

In the city, people stood at the king's gate. They saw the wild geese pass over. They saw the turtle clinging to the stick by his teeth.

"Look! Look!" cried the people. "A turtle in the air! I have never seen a turtle fly until now!"

"And you never will again!" the turtle cried back at them.

As he spoke, he let go of the stick. Down, down, down he fell, to dash and crash and smash on the stone steps of the king's gate.

King Cackle went out to look at what was left of the turtle. The wise man went with him.

King Cackle said to the wise man, "Wise Sir, why did the turtle fall?"

"Sir," said the wise man, "you joked that I should tell you the next time I saw bad things come of talking at the wrong time. This is that next time. The turtle spoke at the wrong time. So he came to a bad end."

"So the turtle, too, was a King Cackle?" said King Cackle. "I see I must change my ways."

And he tried so hard to change his ways that he lost his nickname. And in time he grew into a wise king, who spoke only at the right time.

The Monkey and the Pea

There was once a king with rich lands. Yet he made up his mind to go out with his men and win a poor land.

A wise man said to him, "Sir, do not go. You have enemies who will take your rich lands when you go to win this poor one. You will have lost a lot to get little."

"I will go anyway," said the king.

So he set out with all his men. The wise man went with him, too.

At the end of the first day, the king's men made a camp among the trees. They lit fires, and set pots of water on them, to cook rice and peas to eat.

A monkey hung by one arm from a tree, to look with big eyes at the peas.

Then he sprang down, to grab them. Both hands were full of

peas. Then he sprang back, and sat down in the tree, to eat them.

As he ate, a pea fell out of one of his hands.

So he threw away all the peas he held in both hands; and down he sprang from the tree, to hunt for his lost pea.

To and fro, to and fro he went. His little hands slid under the grass and twigs.

But he did not find his lost pea.

At last he went back to his tree. Now he had no peas at all.

He sat still, with a sad look on his face.

The king had seen all this.

So now he said to the wise man, "Wise Sir, what did you think of that?"

And the wise man told him,

"Sir, I have seen this twice today.

A king who throws rich lands away

To win a poor one – is not he

Just like this monkey with his pea?"

The king stood still, to think.

Then he said, "Yes, wise Sir. I am."

And he went back, with all his men, to keep his rich lands safe.

Old Riddles

1. Little Nancy Etticoat with a white petticoat,

   And a red nose;

   The longer she stands, the shorter she grows.

2. On a far hill there is a red deer,

   The more you shoot it, the more you may,

   You can't drive that red deer away.

3. As I went over London Bridge

   Upon a cloudy day

   I met a fellow clothed in yellow.

   I took him up and sucked his blood,

   And threw his skin away.

4.   In marble halls as white as milk,

     Lined with a skin as soft as silk,

     Within a fountain crystal clear,

     A golden apple does appear.

     No doors are there to this stronghold,

     Yet thieves break in and steal the gold.

5.   White bird featherless

     Flew from Paradise,

     Pitched on the castle wall;

     Along came Lord Landless,

     Took it up handless

     And rode away horseless

     To the king's white hall.

(answers over the page...)

Answers to the riddles

1. A candle

2. The rising sun

3. A blood-orange

4. An egg

5. Snow and the sun

Further Reading

More books by Isabel Wyatt:
The Eight-Year-Old Legend Book
Homer's Odyssey
The Kingdom of Beautiful Colours and Other Stories
    (previously *The Book of Fairy Princes*)
Legends of King Arthur
Magical Wonder Tales: King Beetle Tamer and Other Stories
Norse Hero Tales: The King and the Green Angelica and Other Stories
The Seven-Year-Old Wonder Book

More story anthologies for children:
Celtic Wonder Tales and Other Stories by Ella Young
Christ Legends (previously *The Emperor's Vision*) by Selma Lagerlöf
An Illustrated Treasury of Hans Christian Andersen's Fairy Tales, illustrated by
    Anastasia Archipova
A Journey Through Time in Verse and Rhyme by Heather Thomas
The King of Ireland's Son by Padraic Colum
An Illustrated Treasury of Scottish Folk and Fairy Tales by Theresa Breslin
An Illustrated Treasury of Grimm's Fairy Tales, illustrated by Daniela Drescher
Mary's Little Donkey and the Escape to Egypt by Gunhild Sehlin
Milon and the Lion by Jakob Streit
Myths of the World by Padraic Colum
One Thousand and One Nights, illustrated by Olga Dugina
*Over the Hills and Far Away: Stories of Dwarfs, Fairies, Gnomes and Elves
    From Around Europe*, illustrated by Daniela Drescher
Stories of the Saints by Siegwart Knijpenga
Swedish Folk Tales, illustrated by John Bauer
Tales from African Dreamtime by Magdalene Sacranie